Benjamin Cronyn

A Charge delivered to the Clergy of the Diocese of Huron

SALZWASSER
VERLAG

Benjamin Cronyn

A Charge delivered to the Clergy of the Diocese of Huron

Reprint of the original, first published in 1859.

1st Edition 2022 | ISBN: 978-3-37512-790-9

Verlag (Publisher): Salzwasser Verlag GmbH, Zeilweg 44, 60439 Frankfurt, Deutschland
Vertretungsberechtigt (Authorized to represent): E. Roepke, Zeilweg 44, 60439 Frankfurt, Deutschland
Druck (Print): Books on Demand GmbH, In de Tarpen 42, 22848 Norderstedt, Deutschland

A CHARGE

DELIVERED TO THE

CLERGY OF THE DIOCESE

OF

HURON,

IN

ST. PAUL'S CATHEDRAL, LONDON,

CANADA WEST,

AT

HIS PRIMARY VISITATION, IN JUNE, 1859,

BY

BENJAMIN CRONYN, D.D.,

LORD BISHOP OF HURON.

.

TORONTO:
ROWSELL & ELLIS.
1859.

[PRICE ONE SHILLING.]

A CHARGE,

&c., &c.

My Reverend Brethren,

I feel deeply, more deeply than I can express, the solemn position which I occupy when in the discharge of my duty as a chief minister in the Church of God, I am called to counsel you upon subjects of the deepest interest and of vital importance. I would therefore seek an interest in your prayers, that the Great Head of the Church may be with me by His Spirit on this trying occasion, and may enable me to discharge this duty to the glory of His name and to the good of His Church.

When addressing you for the first time as your Diocesan, my mind naturally reverts to my predecessor in the Episcopal office—to him who, for so many years, presided over the Diocese of Toronto before its division. We who have long known him, and have learned to entertain for him a strong filial affection, must rejoice that, though this part of the Diocese has been removed from under his wise and energetic government, he still continues in the full enjoyment of his mental and bodily powers, to preside over that portion of the Diocese of Toronto which still remains under his Episcopal jurisdiction. We trust and pray that he may be long spared to discharge the duties of his office with the energy and firmness which have always characterized him, and that when his appointed time here is spent, and the silver cord is loosed, he may be found prepared, through the merits of Christ, to partake, with all the redeemed of God, of that Crown of Righteousness which the Lord the righteous judge will bestow upon all them that love his appearing.

Nor can we fail, at this our first meeting, to call to mind with much sadness of heart, the severe loss with which it has pleased God to visit us by the removal from among us of one who had taken a lively interest in the erection of this Diocese, and who had strenuously laboured to bring about this event. The late Dr. Evans, who had been a faithful missionary in this country for over 30 years, was just spared to see his long cherished hope of an increase of the Episcopate in Upper Canada realized, when it pleased the Great Head of the Church to call him from the trials and the warfare of the Church Militant here below to a participation in the joys of the Church Triumphant above.

While we who were privileged to enjoy his acquaintance, and to partake of Communion with a Christian Brother of such sincere and unaffected piety, and of such enlarged experience in the things of God, must ever mourn his loss, still, we submit, without repining, to the dispensation which has deprived us of the presence of one we so much loved, being assured that he who ordereth all things in the Church cannot err, and that to our dear Brother to depart and be with Christ was far better than to remain with the tried and tempted children of men here below. To us who were his cotemporaries or his seniors, his removal cannot fail to suggest a striking warning to work while it is called to-day, for the night cometh when no man can work. His widow and his orphans are amongst us, and I feel assured that those who knew, and so highly valued our departed brother, need not to be reminded of the duty which rests upon them to watch over, with paternal solicitude, those objects of his fondest earthly love, and above all, continually to bear them upon their hearts at a throne of grace, that the Father of the fatherless, and the friend of the widow may be their God and guide, their sun and their shield, that he may give them grace here and glory hereafter, for Christ's sake.

I have deferred calling you together, my Reverend Brethren, until I should have had the opportunity of becoming personally acquainted with every section of the country, and might thus be in possession of such information as would assist us in devising plans for the welfare of our Church, and for the propagation of the Gospel in the Diocese.

I had known something of the state and spiritual necessities of the country before I entered upon the duties of the Episcopate, and a personal acquaintance with the remote parts of the Diocese has confirmed in me the conviction, that unless great and strenuous efforts are made to send missionaries into those parts of the Diocese which have been so long neglected, the members of our communion, who are now numerous in the country, will shortly be necessitated to attach themselves and their families to some other christian body, and thus become lost to our Church for ever. It cannot be expected that men situated as many of our people are, in places where they cannot enjoy the religious privileges to which they have been accustomed at home, should from year to year retain their attachment to the Church of their fathers, and refuse to unite themselves with those in their neighbourhood who exhibit a zeal for religion, and a desire to benefit the souls of men. At first, perhaps, the religious meetings in their neighbourhood, to which they are warmly invited, are attended reluctantly, but, in a little time, their minds become affected with what they continually hear and behold, and they are led to regard first with coldness, and in the end with prejudice, the Church to which, on their arrival in the country, they were devotedly attached. This process has for years been going on in various parts of the Diocese. I trust that, with the Divine blessing upon our labours, we may be enabled in some degree to stop the progress of the evil. But in order to accomplish this, greater efforts than have ever yet been made, must be put forth by us and by the Church at large.

I gladly avail myself of this opportunity of our first meeting together, to set before you, my Reverend Brethren, my views concerning the condition of the Diocese, and of our duty to make every effort to meet and counteract the evil which has long prevailed amongst us. I should hope that I may, before we separate, be enabled to ascertain the opinions of the Clergy upon the same subjects, many of whom, by their long experience, and by their intimate knowledge of the country, are well qualified to advise as to the best mode of proceeding under our present circumstances. I do not then desire merely to express my own views and opinions on the present occasion, but to take counsel with you, my Brethren in the Ministry, and to avail myself of the knowledge and experience which I know many of you possess. Let us lift up our hearts to the Giver of every good and perfect gift, that He may be present with us by His Spirit, so that all our deliberations may be begun, continued and ended in His name and to His praise.

Another reason why I have greatly deferred this meeting is, not only that we may by mutual advice assist each other, but that we can, by taking sweet counsel together concerning the truth of God, stir each other up to more faith in Christ, more devotedness to His service, and more love for the souls of men. As we shall be together for the greater part of this week, I should hope, that not only the public business of the Church will engage our attention, but that we shall be enabled to redeem some portions of the time which might otherwise be lost, and to devote them to religious exercises—to the reading of God's word, to prayer for the Divine blessing upon ourselves and those committed to our care, and to such Christian communion as may promote our growth in grace and in the knowledge of our Lord and Saviour Jesus Christ.

Before entering upon the more immediate consideration of the circumstances of our own portion of the Church, I would briefly glance at the condition of the world at the present time. The signs of the times must always be a subject of the deepest interest to the Christian man. We behold that portion of the earth which has from the earliest days of Christianity enjoyed the blessings of civilization and a preached gospel, now convulsed with war—that most severe vial of Divine displeasure is again poured forth upon the platform of the old Roman Empire—the seat of the beast is again visited by one of those scourges with which God, in his holy word, has declared he will punish men for sin. We have been fondly hoping, since the Paris Conference, that peace would prevail for many years in Europe, but on a sudden we behold war with all its horrors inflicted upon that portion of the earth, and we are almost at a loss to assign the cause, or to discover an adequate reason, for the mustering of such hosts to the battle as we now see engaged in mutual destruction on the plains of Italy. The events which are now taking place in Christendom may be the appointed means whereby God will bring about the destruction of the man of sin, the final overthrow of the mystical Babylon foredoomed of God, which we know he will accomplish in due time. We behold also the progressive drying up of the great river Euphrates, in other words, the decrease of the Turkish power, as foretold in the revelation of God; and a spirit of enquiry into the truth of Christianity is manifested among the Jewish people more extensively than at any former period of their history; and those nations of the earth, which, up to the present time, have been entirely closed against the introduction of God's Word, are now prepared for its reception; so that we may in imagination conceive the Angel of the Revelation flying "in the midst of Heaven, having the everlasting gospel to preach unto them that dwell on the earth, and to every nation and kindred, and tongue, and people." These signs of the times, (we would speak with all humility) appear to indicate that "the Lord is about to make bare His holy arm in the eyes of all the nations," and to establish the kingdom of Christ upon the ruins of all those earthly kingdoms which have existed in the world.

In entering upon the subject of our own Diocese, I think it desirable to lay before you such statistical information as may enable you to form just ideas concerning the position and the wants of our Church in this part of Canada.

When the division of the former Diocese of Toronto took place, thirteen counties were separated from it, and became the Diocese of Huron. These counties comprise the western part of what was formerly known as Upper Canada. They contain 137 townships, averaging 144 square miles each, many of which have only recently been surveyed, and are now rapidly filling with settlers from Great Britain and Ireland, and from the North American Colonies. The Diocese is an irregular figure, extending from east to west about 180 miles, and from north to south about 190 miles. It contains as nearly as it can be estimated about 20,000 square miles, by far the greater part of which is fertile land available for agricultural purposes. The population is at present calculated at 402,581, a large proportion of these are members of the United Church of England and Ireland, and there are many who belong to no Christian body, who have never attached themselves to any Church. Amongst this latter class there is a wide field for missionary exertion. The entire number of the Clergy in the Diocese, including the Bishop, the Parochial Clergy, Travelling Missionaries, Missionaries to the Indians and the fugitive slaves, is fifty-seven. This comprises two superannuated Clergymen, and one master of a country grammar school.

At the time of the division of the Diocese of Toronto there were forty-three Clergymen in this section of it, seven have been received since from other Dioceses, and fifteen ordained, making a total of sixty-five. But we are to set against this seven who have left the Diocese, and one removed by death, leaving the present number of the Clergy fifty-seven. If we subtract from this number nineteen who are exclusively occupied in towns and villages, two superannuated Clergymen, and one master of a grammar school, it leaves thirty-five Missionaries to minister to our brethren scattered through 137 townships, to seek to bring the Gospel to the Aborigines of the country who look to us for instruction, and to labour amongst the fugitive slaves, who have taken refuge in this country, many of whom are as ignorant of Christ and His salvation as their brethren who yet remain in heathen darkness on the Continent of Africa. Since April, 1858, I have visited eighty-four congregations in the Diocese, and preached 130 sermons; I have confirmed 1,453 candidates, consecrated five churches and two burial grounds, ordained fifteen Deacons and three Priests, and travelled in the discharge of these duties 2,452 miles. It ased God that, for some time last autumn, my duties were interrupted by an attack of remittent fever, which confined me for several weeks; however, during the past winter, I was able to visit the northern part of the Diocese, and, though the disease has returned this spring in the form of ague, I hope, through the Divine blessing, I shall be enabled to visit several Missions where candidates for confirmation have been prepared and where my presence is required. It is well to state, as many may be ignorant of the fact, that there are within the limits of this Diocese, and conducted by our Clergy, five Missions to the Aborigines.* Two of these have been supported for many years by the New England Society, and have conferred incalculable blessings upon the remnant of the Six Nations, once so famous in the annals of the country. Last July I visited both these Missions, and was truly gratified with what I witnessed amongst this interesting people. I confirmed at St. Paul's Church, in the Mohawk village on the Grand River, fifty-eight candidates; and at St. John's Church, Tuscarora, forty-three candidates. The success which has attended the labours of the Missionaries in both these settlements, proves that well directed efforts faithfully persevered in, will, with the Divine blessing, succeed with the

---

* See Appendix, Note A.

nativ Indians of this continent; and that, notwithstanding all that learned infidelity may say to the contrary, the blessings of civilization and Christianity may be enjoyed by them equally as by their white brethren.* The Mission on Walpole Island furnishes another proof, that they, who sow in faith and patience amongst the Indians, shall reap if they faint not. I visited the Island in October, and confirmed forty candidates. This Mission, it is to be feared, will be discontinued, as I have been informed that the assistance heretofore given by the Government is about to be withdrawn. I have made application to some of the societies in England, and I hope that something will be done towards supporting this and the other Missions to the Aborigines, which are similarly circumstanced.† There is a Mission to the Muncey town and Oneida Indians, on the river Thames, which I regret to say is placed in the same position with that on Walpole Island. The small salary heretofore given to the Missionary is about to be withdrawn, and the Mission will be allowed to lapse altogether, if funds are not provided by Christian benevolence to sustain it. I visited both the stations of this Mission in August last, and confirmed fifteen candidates. There are no Pagans now remaining among the Muncey Indians, all profess Christianity, and many of them adorn their profession by a blameless life and godly conversation. A few Pagans are still found among the Oneidas, but we hope the day is not far distant when they too shall be added to the Church.‡ Surely the remnant of the tribes which once possessed the vast forests around us, from one of which we have borrowed the name by which our Diocese is known, should call forth our Christian sympathy, and we should never cease to labour and plead in their behalf, until every trace of Pagan superstition has been eradicated from amongst them, and they have been made partakers of the fulness of the blessings of the Gospel of Christ.§

---

* See Appendix, note B.   ‡ See Appendix, note D.
† See Appendix, note C.   § See Appendix, note E.

In order to meet, in some degree, the spiritual wants of the Diocese, it will be necessary that the members of the Church should strenuously exert themselves, and liberally contribute of their substance "as the Lord has prospered them." Our Church Society, which is now incorporated and capable of holding and administering the funds contributed by the people for religious purposes, furnishes the most suitable channel through which the religious offerings of the people may be poured into the treasury of the Lord. By its constitution it is open to all the members of our Church. The contribution of £1 5s. per annum qualifies the donor to be elected a member of the Corporation, and all the business of the Society is transacted at open meetings, where every incorporated member is entitled to be present, and to take part in all the proceedings.

The peculiar organization of the Society renders it eminently fitted to keep the wants of the Diocese before the minds of our people, and to remind them from time to time of their duty towards their fellow men and fellow Christians. The four quarterly sermons to be preached in every Church and station in the Diocese furnish opportunities to the Clergy to bring before their congregations in the most unexceptionable way, and to press upon them their duty to give of their substance to promote the cause of God in the land. And the Annual Meeting of each Parochial Association, enables the advocates of the Society to stir up the minds of the people by setting before them the progress which the Society has made, and the necessity which still exists for exertion on the part of the members of the Church. Heretofore the collections made for our Society, with the exception of one, have been devoted to the missionary cause. This being the most urgent want felt in all parts of the Diocese. But we hope that ere long the Society will be placed in a position to take up some, if not all, of the other excellent objects proposed in its constitution.

I would, therefore, press upon the Clergy the necessity of

supporting the Church Society of the Diocese, by every means in their power ; upon it, in a very great degree, under God, depends the success of our efforts for the propagation of the Gospel amongst the people, and the supply of additional missionaries to labour in those parts of the Diocese where the people are as yet unable to support their own Clergymen. Were we required only to meet and provide for the natural increase of the population in the older settlements of the Diocese, I think this might be effected through the efforts of the Church Society. But inasmuch as large numbers of the adult emigrants are yearly introduced into the Diocese from Great Britain and Ireland, it has become an imperative duty to apply to religious societies at home to assist us in providing the means of grace for their poor fellow countrymen who yearly come amongst us. The Society for the Propagation of the Gospel has granted £400 sterling per annum for the support of missionaries in that new tract of country which lies at the northern and western extremity of the Diocese. This grant is only for three years, but we hope that when the real state of the country is known to that benevolent society, which has, for so many years, liberally contributed to the wants of Canada, the grant will not only be extended, but enlarged. By the kind liberality of the Society for Promoting Christian Knowledge, I have been enabled to assist in the completion of 15 Churches in the Diocese, and a second grant of £300, which I have just received from the same venerable body, places it in my power to render assistance to several new Churches which are being erected in remote parts of the Diocese. The Service Books and Prayer Books granted by the same Society have been most gratefully received. The Colonial Church and School Society has also contributed towards the supply of our necessities, and I desire to express my deep sense of the valuable assistance which I have received from that excellent Society. The Mission to the Fugitive Slaves in Canada, which is conducted under the auspices of this Society, carries on its operations within the limits of this Diocese, and every well wisher of our race will rejoice to learn, that enlightened and well directed efforts are made to bring the knowledge of salvation to this downtrodden people.

So long as slavery is upheld by the laws of the neighbouring republic, so long will the degraded and enslaved African, who hears of Canada as a land of freedom and a refuge from cruelty and oppression, seek to escape from a country in which the first rights of manhood are denied him, and to reach these shores, where, sheltered beneath the flag under which no slave can live, he may carry himself erect as an immortal being, and experience the protection of those laws which recognize no difference between man and man, but extend to all whom God has created in his own image, the privileges which belong alike to all the heirs of immortality.

Having now set before you, my Reverend Brethren, such statistical statements as I conceive to be necessary at the present time, and having briefly glanced at some other subjects of interest, I will proceed, humbly invoking the Divine blessing, to direct your attention to some questions of a purely spiritual character, the consideration of which may be profitable to us all.

And, first, with reference to the high and holy office which has been committed to us. This office is thus described in the exhortation of the Bishop to such as are admitted to the higher order of the Ministry in our Church, in which we find the following solemn words, " And now again we exhort you in the name of our Lord Jesus Christ, that you have in remembrance into how high a dignity, and to how weighty an office and charge ye are called, that is to say, to be Messengers, Watchmen, and Stewards of the Lord : to teach and to premonish, to feed and provide for the Lord's family, to seek for Christ's sheep that are dispersed abroad, and for His children who are in the midst of this naughty world, that they may be saved through Christ for ever." Here we have in most impressive words the sacred office of a Christian Minister fully described. It differs, most essentially, from the office of the Priesthood under the Mosaic dispensation, and should never be confounded with it.

Under the law, Aaron and his descendants were ordained to offer gifts and sacrifices for the people, these things were a figure for the time then present. But this office has ceased for ever under the Christian dispensation. Aaron, in all that he did, was a type of our Great High Priest, and all the sacrifices which he offered looked forward to, and were terminated in, that one great sacrifice which Christ, as our surety and representative, offered up to God. The Apostle Paul, in his Epistle to the Hebrews, clearly teaches that the "Priesthood being changed, there is of necessity made a change of the Law." That Christ, our Great High Priest, hath an unchangeable Priesthood—that is, a Priesthood which passeth not from one to another—that by one offering of Himself once offered, He has for ever perfected them that are sanctified—that therefore there remaineth no more sacrifice for sin," and that, having entered within the Holiest of all, even Heaven itself, Christ, our representative, is there, ever ready to fulfil His Priestly office for his people—to present His own blood in their behalf, and to make continual and prevalent intercession for them.

The great sin of the Roman Apostacy is, that it interferes with, and encroaches upon, the office of Him "who abideth a Priest for ever;" that it dishonours the Priesthood and sacrifice of the Lord Jesus Christ, intruding sinful and fallible men into a participation of the former, and placing the latter on a level with those sacrifices of the law which needed daily to be repeated, and which could never take away sin. And that instead of inviting and encouraging men to come with boldness to a throne of Grace, through our Great High Priest who is passed into the Heavens, it interposes men of like passions with others, between the sinner and the Saviour, and makes the Priest, instead of a Messenger, Watch

man and Steward of the Lord, a judicial dispenser of absolution and salvation to his fellow sinners. Hence have
arisen many of the unscriptural doctrines of the Church of
Rome. Because of this false assumption on the part of the
Priesthood, auricular confession and priestly absolution have
been introduced; penances and self-inflicted torments have
been resorted to as an atonement for sin; and purgatory,
with its thousands of years of torments, which are repre-
sented as being as bad as those of hell, has been brought in
to finish the work of purification which that precious blood,
"which cleanseth from all sin,' alone can effect.

We can never be sufficiently thankful, my Brethren in the
Ministry, that, at the glorious Reformation, our Church was
delivered from this, among so many other delusions of the
wicked one; that the true character of the Christian Ministry
was vindicated, and our Lord was restored to that office,
which He alone can fill; "the only and all sufficient Priest
of his Church and people." Let us ever bear in mind that
we are Ambassadors for Christ, that we have the ministry of
reconciliation committed to us. "To wit, that God was in
Christ reconciling the world unto Himself, not imputing
their trespasses unto them, and hath committed unto us the
word of reconciliation," and, that, therefore it is our duty to
make the godly determination not to know any thing amongst
the people over whom we are placed but for "Jesus Christ
and him crucified." As Messengers then we are faithfully to
exhibit the word of reconciliation. We are to invite sinners
to be reconciled to God. We are to proclaim the Gospel to
every creature. We are to set forth the record that "God
hath given to us eternal life, and this life is in his Son." In
order that this duty may be efficiently discharged, we must
have our own minds duly impressed with the saving truths
of the Gospel. How can a man entreat sinners to be
reconciled to God, who has not experienced this reconciliation in his own soul? How can a man press the acceptance
of the record of God concerning Christ upon others, who

has not embraced that record with a living faith? It is indeed a melancholy position for a man to occupy, to be a Minister of Christ, but not a real Christian. The external call to the ministry which we have received according to primitive order, only confers official authority; the internal call is the true Divine vocation without which no man can really perform with effect the office of a Messenger of Christ. What can be more solemn than the question put by the Bishop at the ordination of a Deacon in our Church? "Do you trust that you are inwardly moved by the Holy Ghost to take upon you this office?" Bishop Burnet, remarking upon this, says, "Certainly the answer that is made to this ought to be well considered, for if any says ' I trust so,' that yet knows nothing of any such motion, he lies to the Holy Ghost, and makes his first approach to the altar with a lie in his mouth, and that not to men but to God." My Reverend Brethren, there is such a thing as being outwardly a Minister of Christ, it may be even for many years, without any vital union with him, who is the fountain of all grace; "the head over all things to the Church." Such Ministers may well be compared to clouds without water, no fructifying blessing descends upon the people through their means. That portion of the field, upon which their shadow rests, is rendered unproductive of spiritual fruit, no harvest is gathered into the garner of the Lord. Bishop Bull has well said, " The Priest who is not clothed with righteousness, though otherwise richly adorned with all the ornaments of human and divine literature, and those gilded over with the rays of seraphic prudence, is yet but a naked beggarly and despicable creature, of no authority, no interest, no use, no service in the Church of God." For the due discharge of our ministry, we are therefore called, in the first place, to take heed unto ourselves and to the state of our own souls. Archbishop Leighton, in a sermon to the clergy, fully and faithfully treats this subject. He says, "We think, that they who savingly know not Christ, should not be fit to make other men acquainted with him. He that can tell men what God has done for his own soul, is the likeliest to bring their souls to God; hardly can he speak to the heart who speaks not from it; again, how can a frozen hearted preacher warm his hearers' hearts, and enkindle them with the love of God? But he whom the love of Christ constrains, his lively recommendations of Christ, and speeches of love, shall sweetly constrain others to love him. Above all loves, it is most true of this, that none can speak sensible of it, but those that have felt it." There is a great danger, my Reverend Brethren, that from constant habit of speaking and preaching upon divine subjects, our own personal religion may be neglected, that we may be tempted to rest satisfied with what has been well called, "a professional piety." Often the minister who appears warm and energetic in the pulpit is cold and formal in his private devotions. This should be guarded against, we should endeavour to maintain communion with God, in the reading of His word, in meditation upon it and in prayer, that so we may speak out of the abundance of the heart, when we undertake to fulfil the office of Messengers of Christ. The words of Archbishop Leighton, upon this point also, are most valuable: "Upright, meek, humble, and heavenly minds, then, must the Ambassadors of this great King have, and so obtain His intimacy; mounting upon those wings of prayer and meditation, and having the eye of faith upwards. Thus shall they learn more of His choicest mysteries in one hour, than by many days poring upon casuists, school-men and such like. This ought to be done, I confess, but above all the other must not be omitted. Their chief study should be that of their commission, the Holy Scriptures; the way to speak skilfully from God is often to hear him speak." But we are also Watchmen, and in the discharge of this duty we are to be faithful, placing before men their danger, their ruined and lost state by nature, and warning them to flee from the wrath to come. We are to use great plainness of speech, testifying to all

c

"repentance towards God, and faith in our Lord Jesus Christ;" setting before all alike that "if any man have not the spirit of Christ he is none of his," that, "unless a man be born again he cannot see the kingdom of God." These truths faithfully declared, will not be acceptable to the natural man, but we are bound to perform the part of faithful watchmen, whether the people will hear, or whether they will forbear, our warning must therefore be given with no uncertain sound, we must "declare all the counsel of God," that "we may be pure from the blood of all men." This office of Watchmen we are to perform with all love, with an earnest desire for the salvation of souls, in "meekness instructing them which oppose themselves, if God peradventure will grant them repentance to the acknowledgment of the truth." As Stewards, it is required that a man be found faithful, St. Paul (in 1 Cor. IV., 12,) says, "Let a man so account of us as Ministers of Christ and Stewards of the Mysteries of God." As we have been allowed of God to be put in trust with the Gospel, it becomes us faithfully to dispense it; like the great Apostle of the Gentiles, we are to keep back nothing that is profitable to the people. He could not surely be regarded as a faithful Steward of the Mysteries of God, who would deliberately suppress any part of Divine truth committed to him. Following the example of our blessed Lord and His Apostles, the faithful Steward of Christ will endeavour, that every thing which God has revealed in his Holy Word for the instruction of men, shall in due measure be presented to them. Thus only can he "fulfil the ministry which he has received of the Lord Jesus, to testify the Gospel of the grace of God."

Amongst the many means of grace which God has appointed in the Church, and in the diligent use of which we are to fulfil the duties of Messengers, Watchmen, and Stewards of the Lord, the preaching of the word stands pre-eminent. The pulpit is the Minister's great battle-field.. There he conquers, or is overcome. And, here, I would address myself more particularly to my young brethren. It is of the utmost importance that you should give all diligence to prepare yourselves for the efficient discharge of this most important part of your ministerial duty. The exhortations of St. Paul to Timothy, concerning his ministry at Ephesus, show us what a prominent place he assigns to the preaching of the word; in the 4th chap. of the 1st Epistle to Timothy he thus writes: "Till I come, give attendance to reading, to exhortation to doctrine, neglect not the gift that is in thee, which was given thee by prophecy, with the laying on of the hands of the Presbytery, meditate on these things, give thyself wholly to them, that thy profiting may appear to all, take heed unto thyself, and unto the doctrine; continue in them, for in doing this thou shalt both save thyself and them that hear thee;" and again: "study to show thyself approved unto God, a workman that needeth not to be ashamed rightly dividing the word of truth;" and again, in this most solemn address which we find towards the close of the 2nd Epistle: "I charge thee, therefore, before God and the Lord Jesus Christ, who shall judge the quick and the dead at his appearing, and his kingdom, preach the word, be instant in season, and out of season, reprove, rebuke, exhort with all long suffering and doctrine." From these, amongst many similar passages from the writings of the Apostles, we learn what a high value he set upon the ordinance of preaching. He evidently recognised it as God's ordinary means for the conversion of sinners, and the edification of saints. It has been well said by an able writer of our day: "Of all the methods of diffusing religion, preaching is the most efficient. It is to preaching Christianity owes its origin, its continuance, and its progress." Our blessed Lord in his last interview with his disciples, thus delivered to them their commission: "Go ye into all the world and preach the Gospel to every creature, he that believeth and is baptised shall be saved, but he that believeth not shall be damned." And we read, that in compliance with this command, "They went forth and preached every where, the Lord working with them, and confirming the word with signs following." Preaching, then, must be regarded by the Christian minister as the primary instrument, in the Divine economy, for the gathering in of Christ's sheep, that are dispersed abroad, and for the edification of his children who are in the midst of this naughty world. Hooker has thus described this ordinance : " So worthy a part of Divine service we should greatly wrong, if we did not esteem preaching as the blessed ordinance of God, sermons as keys to the Kingdom of Heaven, as wings to the soul, as spurs to the good affections of men, unto the sound and healthy as food, as physic unto diseased minds." It becomes the minister of Christ, then, to spare no labour to fit and prepare himself for the efficient discharge of this duty. It is indeed a solemn, nay a most awful position, which the ambassador of Christ occupies when he stands before the people to deliver to them a message from his Lord, upon the reception or rejection of which their eternal destiny depends. Placed in such a position, how careful should he be to speak as the oracles of God, not to waste the precious moments which he spends in the pulpit upon a vain display of fine speaking, or fine writing, or upon the discussion of subjects of mere wordly interest, or upon foolish and unlearned questions which gender strife, and which are after the traditions of men, after the rudiments of the world, and not after Christ. I shall now offer a few remarks as to the manner and matter of our Sermons, not with the hope that I shall be able to add any thing to what has already been written, upon subjects which have exercised the minds, and engaged the pens, of some of the most pious and devoted men in every age of our Church since the Reformation, but that these things may be more solemnly impressed upon our souls. As to the manner of preaching, much difference of opinion prevails. There are some who think that sermons read to the people are not calculated to produce any saving or lasting effect upon the hearers. That, however sound they may be as to their doctrine, however accurate in their style and composition, and however well and logically arranged, they fail to reach the heart, and to affect the consciences of the great mass of the people. They argue that it requires all the appliances of the eye, voice, and action to arrest and retain the attention of men, who, for the most part, are unaccustomed to fix their thoughts, for any length of time, upon subjects of a purely intellectual or spiritual character, and that therefore the reading of sermons from the pulpit should be altogether forbidden, or, at least, discontinued as much as possible. On the other hand, there are those who equally condemn the practice of what is commonly called extempore preaching, who say that sermons delivered without book, must, of necessity, be always crude and ill-digested. That those who adopt this habit are strongly tempted to give way to sloth, and in all probability will continually repeat themselves, and though the text may be varied, will substantially always preach the same sermon. Experience convinces us that truth lies between these extremes; we have known preachers who invariably wrote and read their sermons, who were eminently blessed of God in their ministry, and who were made the instruments of turning many sinners from darkness to light, and from the power of Satan unto God.

While we have known others, and these not a few, who always preached without a written sermon, upon whose ministry the Divine seal has been most abundantly set, and to whom many souls have been given for their hire. If there is, upon the part of the preacher, much study, meditation and prayer, if he draws from the resources of a mind richly stored with Divine truth, and enlightened by the Spirit of God, his sermons, whether written or not, will be acknowledged of God, and the Divine promise will be fulfilled, which says, "So shall my word be that goeth forth out of My mouth, it shall not return unto Me void; but it shall accomplish that which I please, and it shall prosper in the thing whereto I sent it." In speaking of extempore preaching, I would not be misunderstood, as though I used the word in the literal sense. It can only be regarded as irreverent in the highest degree, or as most awfully presumptuous, in any man to stand up, as an Ambassador of Christ, and to trust to the impulse of the moment, or to a natural fluency of speech for the message which he is to deliver to the people. I would warn you, my Brethren in the Ministry, against such an irreverent and unbecoming practice. There may be some who imagine that, because they possess much self-confidence, and are not affected by that constitutional nervousness and timidity, which often render the truly pious and humble man embarrassed before the people, they may trust to a natural readiness of expression, and neglect laborious preparation for the pulpit. It should ever be borne in mind that there is such a thing as a vicious fluency of speech; that sound without sense cannot benefit the hearers, and that the tongue may often run rapidly, because it carries no weight either of thought or reflection. Such preaching is unworthy of the name. And while I would encourage my younger Brethren to cultivate the habit of preaching without a written sermon, as the mode most likely to render their ministry acceptible and profitable to their hearers, I would impress upon them the necessity of "being diligent in prayers and in the reading of the Holy Scriptures, and in such studies as help to the knowledge of the same, laying aside the study of the world and the flesh." Upon this subject, an eminent writer of our own day thus expresses himself, "A most erroneous notion prevails of the easiness of this attainment. A collection of words is often mistaken for a justly defined sentiment, and fluency of utterance is considered to be either indicative of solidity of thought or a fair amends for its deficiency. Now, such an extemporaneous faculty can bring no substantial instruction to our people. Our subject must be studied till it is understood, digested and felt. For a well conducted habit we need not impulse or fluency merely, but a furniture of solid knowledge, combined with simplicity of style ; solid as well as animated manner ; and—*instar omnium*—a mind deeply enriched with the unsearchable treasure of Scripture. This resource will supply the place of many secondary qualifications, while nothing will compensate for the lack of it." In the discharge of this duty of preaching, the minister of Christ should employ such language as will be most intelligible to all the members of the congregation. There are many in every Christian assembly who have not enjoyed the benefit of a liberal education. The language of the preacher should be such as would easily be understood by them. But is it not often the case that the sermons of our Clergy appear to be intended for the educated alone ? and are nearly as unintelligible to many members of the congregation as the Latin mass is to the illiterate members of the Church of Rome ? Archbishop Whately says concerning a fault in speaking and writing akin to that of which I have just spoken, " Young writers and speakers are apt to fall into a style of ponderous verbosity from the idea that they are adding both perspicuity and force to what is said, when they are only encumbering the sense with a needless load of words. It is not indeed uncommon to hear a speaker of this class mentioned as having a very fine command of language, when perhaps it might be said with more correctness that his language has a command of him ; that is, that he follows a train of words rather than of thought." When we ascend the pulpit let this thought be always uppermost in our minds, that we are the bearers of a message of mercy to sinful men, and that the present may be the last opportunity we shall have of delivering our message to some of those who hear us. Under the influence of such a reflection as this, the minister of Christ will be careful not to waste the precious moments in the pulpit, and so to clothe his ideas in plain speech, that all who, in the Providence of God, are brought within the sound of his voice, may clearly understand the message of mercy which he is commissioned to proclaim. It is indeed a distressing thought that one benighted fellow creature should leave the house of God after listening to Christ's ambassador delivering his message without any clear comprehension of the purport of that which has been spoken in his hearing.

I now pass on from the consideration of the manner of delivering the gospel message to some reflections upon the matter or substance of it. And here, my Reverend Brethren, the word of God is clear. In whatever way the Minister of Christ delivers the message which is entrusted to him, whether by written or by unwritten sermons, by reading God's word, or in any other way, still the message is ever one and the same, the substance of our preaching must be Jesus Christ and him crucified. The Christian Minister should ever bear in mind, that his great aim should be, not to improve the intellects, or gratify the taste of his hearers, but to convert sinners unto God. In our mixed congregations there will always be many who are yet in the gall of bitterness and in the bond of iniquity, and it is only by exalting Christ ond proclaiming Him as the Saviour, that they can be raised up to newness of life. We may set before such the terrors of the Lord, His judgments against sin as denounced in His holy law, but if we fail to exhibit Christ, as the only and all sufficient Saviour, our labour will be in vain. The following passage from the writings of an eminent author of the last age, puts this in a striking light: "Had you the fullest acquaintance that ever man acquired, with the principles and duties of natural religion, both in its regards to God and your fellow-creatures; had you the skill and tongue of an angel, to range all these in their fairest order, to place them in their fullest light, and to pronounce and represent the whole law of God, with such force and splendour, as was done to the Israelites at Mount Sinai : you might perhaps lay the consciences of men under deep conviction (for by the law is the knowledge of sin,) but I am fully persuaded you would never reconcile one soul to

God, you would never change the heart of one sinner, nor bring him into the favour of God, nor fit him for the joys of Heaven, without this blessed Gospel which is committed to your hands." Our blessed Lord declared, "as Moses lifted up the serpent in the wilderness, even so must the Son of Man be lifted up, that whosoever believeth in Him should not perish but have everlasting life," and again, "I, if I be lifted up, will draw all men unto me." For the conversion of sinners, for the edification of Saints, for enforcing holiness of life upon the people of God, and for preparing them for that eternity to which we are all hastening, we should know nothing but Jesus Christ and Him crucified, all our discourses should so centre in Him, that the minds of our hearers should be continually directed to Him. Archbishop Secker, speaking of the falling away of members of the Church to dissent, thus warned his Clergy, "We have in fact lost many of our people to sectaries, by not preaching in a manner sufficiently evangelical, and shall neither recover them from the extravagancies into which they have run; nor keep more from going over to them but by returning to the right way." And Bishop Horne remarks, "Many well-meaning Christians of this time thirst after the doctrine of the Gospel, and think that they have heard nothing unless they have heard of salvation by Jesus Christ, which is what we properly call the Gospel. And if they do not hear it in the discourses from our pulpits, where they expect to hear it, they are tempted to wander in search of it to other places of worship." If therefore we desire to retain our people, and to save souls, we shall be diligent in preaching Christ in all His fulness, and in all His power to save. The loss of the people to sectaries, spoken of by these eminent Prelates as the effect of defective preaching in our pulpits, though deeply to be deplored, is not the greatest evil to be apprehended, precious souls are thus sacrificed, and another Gospel is preached, which is yet not another but a perversion of the Gospel of Christ.

D

Another subject which I esteem of paramount importance, and upon which I desire to occupy your attention for a few minutes, is, the true nature and character of the Church. In the XIX. Article, it is thus described, "The visible Church of Christ, is a congregation of faithful men, in which the pure word of God is preached, and the sacraments be duly ministered according to Christ's ordinance, in all those things that of necessity are requisite to the same, as the Church of Jerusalem, Alexandria, and Antioch have erred; so also the Church of Rome hath erred, not only in their living and manner of ceremonies, but also in the matters of faith. By the use of the term "visible church," it is plainly implied, that while there ever has been, and ever will be, a church on earth visible to mortal eyes, yet that there is, also, a mystical and spiritual body of Christ, the members of which cannot be discernable by man. This is "the general assembly and Church of the first-born which are written or enrolled in Heaven;" the true circumcision "which worship God in the Spirit, rejoice in Christ Jesus, and have no confidence in the flesh." The holy Catholic Church in which we profess our belief in the creeds. The visible Church has been compared by our blessed Lord to a net cast into the sea which gathered of every kind both bad and good; to a field in which both tares and wheat grow together until the harvest; to a vine some of whose branches are unfruitful, and fit only to be burned, while some bring forth fruit and are purged of God, that they may bring forth more fruit. In setting this subject before you, I would adopt the words of the learned and judicious Hooker: "The Church of Christ which we properly term his body mystical, can be but one; neither can that one be sensibly discerned by any man, inasmuch as the parts thereof are some in Heaven already with Christ, (albeit their natural persons be visible,) we do not discern under this property, whereby they are truly and infallibly of that body, only our minds by intellectual conceit are able to apprehend, that such a real body there is, a body collective, because it containeth a large multitude; a body mystical, because the mystery of their conjunction is removed altogether from sense. Whatsoever we read in Scripture concerning the endless love and saving mercy which God sheweth towards His Church, the only proper subject thereof is this Church. Concerning this flock it is, that our Lord and Saviour hath promised: "I give unto them eternal life, and they shall never perish, neither shall any pluck them out of my hands." They who are of this society have such marks and notes of distinction from all others, as are not objects unto our sense; only unto God who seeth their hearts and understandeth all their secret cogitations, unto Him they are clear and manifest. All men knew Nathaniel to be an Israelite. But our Saviour piercing deeper giveth further testimony of Him than men could have done, with certainty, as he did, "Behold an Israelite indeed in whom is no guile." If we profess, as Peter did, that we love the Lord, and profess it in the hearing of men, charity is prone to believe all things, and therefore charitable men are likely to think we do so, as long as they see no proof to the contrary. But that our love is sound and sincere, that it cometh from a pure heart and a good conscience, and a faith unfeigned, who can pronounce, saving only the Searcher of all men's hearts, who alone intuitively doth know in this kind who are His?" This able writer and eminent divine, also puts this question: "Is it then possible that the selfsame men should belong both to the synagogue of Satan, and to the Church of Jesus Christ?" and answers thus: "Unto that Church which is his mystical body, not possible; because that body consisteth of none but only true Israelites, true sons of Abraham, true servants and saints of God. Howbeit of the visible body and Church of Jesus Christ, those may be, and oftentimes are, in respect of the main parts of their outward profession, who in regard to their inward disposition of mind, yea, of external conversation, yea, even of some parts of their very profession, are most worthily both hateful in the sight of God himself, and in the eyes of the sounder part of the visible Church most execrable." And I most fully agree with the same writer, that, "For lack of diligent observing the difference first between the Church of God mystical and visible, then between the visible sound, and corrupted, sometimes more, sometimes less, the oversights are neither few nor light that have been committed." Great practical evil must ever follow from the application of the promises and privileges intended for the members of the Spiritual Church, and addressed in God's word to them alone, to men, who are merely Christians by profession, who only pertain to the outward and visible Church, and who are evidently without Christ, being aliens from the commonwealth of the true Israel, and strangers from the covenant of promise,"—men who are far from God, and to whom pertain not the gracious promises and privileges of the Gospel, but the dreadful denunciations of God's wrath and displeasure against those who continue in sin, and who obey not the Gospel of our Lord Jesus Christ.

The minister who, while many members of his congregation are thus going down the broad road to eternal destruction unconverted, unrenewed, unjustified and unsanctified, leads them to imagine that no change of heart is necessary in them, but that they have only to attend to the religious observances of the Church into which they have been admitted by baptism, to cultivate a fair and respectable appearance before men, and that all will be well at the last, should ponder well the word of the Lord by the prophet Ezekiel, "because, even because they have seduced my people saying, peace, and there was no peace; and one built up a wall, and lo, others daubed it with untempered mortar! Say unto them which daub it with untempered mortar, that it shall fall. Then shall be an overflowing shower, and ye, O great hailstones, shall fall, and a stormy wind shall rend it."

The most established believer, the most pious and devoted servant of Christ, when he looks into his own heart and faithfully compares his life with the holy and spiritual law of God, when he finds that the flesh, with its corruptions and lusts, daily war against his soul ; when he is constrained to cry out with the Apostle, " O wretched man that I am, who shall deliver me from the body of this death," is often tempted to doubt whether he has been made partaker of converting and sanctifying grace, and even when he rejoices, to rejoice with trembling. How much more, then, shall the minister of Christ stand in doubt of the spiritual state of his people when he looks upon his congregation and beholds amongst them many who evidence by their lives that the spirit of Christ is not in them, that they are not " the Epistles of Christ known and read of all men ;" that they have not overcome the world, but that the world daily overcomes them ; that they are walking, not after the spirit, but after the flesh, and setting their affections, not on things above, but on things of this world. Surely, in such a case, it becomes the watchman of the Lord to raise his voice and to testify to those who are thus dead in trespasses and in sins, that, " unless they repent, they shall assuredly perish ;" that though they may belong to the visible Church, if they are not made partakers of the sanctify- ing influence of the Holy Ghost, they shall never sit down with Abraham, Isaac and Jacob in the kingdom of God. The unscriptural mode of addressing mixed congre- gations of professing Christians as alike partakers of the grace of Christ, will act as an opiate to the consciences of the people, and can only have the effect of rendering more profound the spiritual sleep in which so many of them lie.

My Reverend Brethren, I would earnestly press this sub- ject on your most serious and prayerful attention, error here will prove fatal to your real usefulness as Ministers of Christ. Nothing worthy of our high calling is effected unless sinners are converted and brought to Christ for salvation. For this we should study, for this we should labour, and above all, for this we should pray without ceasing. For it is by the

Almighty power of God's Spirit alone that the Gospel is made a savor of life unto life in those who hear it.

I shall now offer a few remarks upon the Articles and Formularies of our Church. At your ordination you were asked, "Are you persuaded that the Holy Scriptures contain sufficiently all doctrines required of necessity for eternal salvation through faith in Jesus Christ? And are you determined out of the said Scriptures to instruct the people committed to your charge, and to teach nothing as required of necessity to eternal salvation, but that which you shall be persuaded may be concluded and proved by the Scripture?" and you replied, "I am so persuaded and have so determined by God's grace." This question and answer are in strict accordance with the VI. Article of our Church, and embody the great Protestant principle which was the basis of the Reformation: that the written word of God is the only rule of faith and practice in the Christian Church. The thirty-nine Articles are not to be regarded as a substitute for or a supplement to God's written word, they are a summary of those doctrines which we believe to be fully contained in that word. If from brevity or obscurity, or any other cause, (for human works are always more or less defective,) an explanation of the Articles or any of them, becomes necessary, we are to have recourse for guidance, direction and explanation to the written word alone. The VI. Article clearly states "that whatsoever is not read therein, nor may be proved thereby, is not to be required of any man, that it should be believed as an article of the Faith," and the first Homily most emphatically teaches us, that "there is no truth nor doctrine necessary for our justification and everlasting salvation, but that is, or may be drawn out of that fountain and well of truth." The Articles of our Church were originally framed for "the avoiding of diversities of opinions, and for the establishing of consent touching true religion," and in the Royal declaration prefixed to them it is declared, "that the Articles of the Church of England do contain the true doctrine of the Church of England agreeable to God's word," and referring to the unhappy differences which then prevailed, we find these strong expressions, "we will that all further curious search be laid aside, and these disputes shut up in God's promises as they be generally set forth to us in Holy Scriptures, and the general meaning of the Articles of the Church of England "according to them," and that no man hereafter shall either print, or preach to draw the article aside any way, but shall submit to it in the plain and full meaning thereof; and shall not put his own sense or "comment to be the meaning of the 'Article, but shall take it in the literal and grammatical sense." The original object then for which the Articles were adopted, and the strong language concerning them which I have just read, prove beyond question that they were intended "when first published," to be the strict and only exposition and standard of the doctrines of the Church of England, from which no departure was allowed, and as they are, at the present time, subscribed by all who are admitted to the Ministry in our Communion, and no authority is given to draw them aside or explain them away, it clearly follows, that we are bound to regard them as the strict, dogmatical and unchangeable expositions of the doctrines of the United Church of England and Ireland. To them, as the only authoritative standard, all differences which may arise on points of doctrine are to be brought. The laws of England recognise the Thirty-nine Articles as "the confession of the true Christian faith, and the doctrine of the Sacraments," thus constituting them the Canon of doctrine of the Church of England. But if we have in the Thirty-nine Articles a standard of doctrine in strict accordance with, and resting on the basis of God's revealed word, we have reason, my Brethren in the Ministry, to rejoice that we have in the Book of Common Prayer a standard of devotion so pure, so spiritual, and so scriptural, that, even our enemies themselves being judges, no material flaw or defect can be found in it. At his ordi-

nation every Clergyman signifies his assent and consent
to the Book of Common Prayer, and declares that "it containeth in it nothing contrary to the word of God, that it
may lawfully so be used, and that he himself will use the
form prescribed in the public prayer and administration of
the Sacraments and no other." Thus we are provided for
our public ministrations, with a form of prayer eminently
calculated to stir up a spirit of devotion in the minds of our
people, and to enable them to pour forth the most earnest
and spiritual aspirations, in language the most appropriate.
All the doctrines of the Gospel upon which the salvation of
the sinner depends, are so interwoven in our services, that
the man who is well acquainted with them, and who uses
them constantly and intelligently, is not likely to be corrupted from the simplicity which is in Christ. Above all,
we have so much of God's word introduced into all our services, and we are so constantly referred to this infallible
source for guidance, both as to life and doctrine, that no
service for Public Worship can be conceived more scriptural.
When we reflect that our Reformers had to arrange a Service for a Clergy not half converted from the errors of the
Church of Rome, and for a people still devotedly attached
to the old formularies to which they had been so long accustomed, we cannot fail to admire the wisdom which was given
to them, whereby they were enabled to effect so difficult and
delicate an object without compromising the great truths of
God's Holy Word. In the preface to the Book of Common
Prayer, it is stated that, "It has always been the wisdom
of the Church of England, ever since the first compiling of
the public Liturgy, to keep the mean between the two extremes of too much stiffness in refusing and of too much
easiness in admitting any variations from it." And we are
reminded in the same preface, that the Book of Common
Prayer is entitled to "such just and favourable construction
as in common equity ought to be allowed to all human writings." An eminent Historian of the Reformation thus

speaks of the alterations made in the Book of Common Prayer in the time of Queen Elizabeth: "For the performance of which service there was great care taken for expunging all such passages in it as might give any scandal or offence to the Popish party, or be urged by them in excuse for their not coming to Church and joining with the rest of the Congregation in God's Public Worship." The language of our Church, then, and of our Historians, concerning the Book of Common Prayer is entirely different from that employed concerning the Articles. A spirit of wisdom and prudence, combined with a strong desire to render the public worship such as to induce those who were still attached to the Church of Rome to attend the public services of the Church, presided over the compilation of the Liturgy, and an equitable construction such as is due to human writings is claimed for the Book of Common Prayer. Whereas the Articles were framed "for the avoidance of diversities in religious opinions," and no departure from them is allowed, but they are to be taken in the strict literal and grammatical sense. We are thus furnished with a Canon of doctrine in the Articles of our Church, and with a manual and standard of devotion in our Book of Common Prayer.

There has been much controversy, as to whether the language of our formularies is to be interpreted by the articles of the Church, or *vice versa*. From what I have now brought before you concerning both these sources of information, it is evident that the Thirty-nine Articles are our *ultima ratio* in all questions of doctrine, and that where any of our formularies are expressed in ambiguous language and appear inconsistent with the plain statements of the articles, we are bound to interpret the former by the latter. It would be most unnatural, I had almost said absurd, to interpret the articles which were agreed upon by the Archbishops and Bishops of the Provinces, and the whole Clergy, for the avoidance of diversities of opinions, and for the establishing of consent touching true religion," by the servi-

E

ces which were framed with the avowed purpose of concili-
ating and comprehending those who held opinions widely
different from each other, and of inducing them to unite in
the public worship of the Church. In addition to this,
changes may be made at any time by sufficient authority in
the forms of Divine worship and the rites and ceremonies
appointed to be used therein, as we find set forth in the
preface to the Book of Common Prayer, where we read,
"so on the other side the particular forms of Divine worship, and the rites and ceremonies appointed to be used
therein being things in their own nature indifferent, and
'alterable,' and so acknowledged, it is but reasonable that
upon weighty and important considerations, according to the
various exigences of times and occasions, such changes and
alterations should be made therein, as to those that are
placed in authority should, from time to time, seem necessary
or expedient."

To submit, then, the articles which are unalterable, and
which no man is to draw aside in any way to the interpreta-
tion of formularies which are declared to be alterable, and
which may undergo change at any time, would be to subvert
the natural and reasonable order of things. In all sciences,
whether mathematical or philosophical, things which are
less clear and are open to discussion, are brought to those
axioms and principles which are fixed and immutable, and
are explained or interpreted by them. So also must it be
in discussions concerning the doctrines of our Church. They
are based on God's written word, and are presented to us in
our articles, and we are bound to try and explain all doctrines by this immutable standard with which we are thus
provided.

And now, my Brethren in the ministry, before I conclude,
I desire to suggest to you a few considerations, which, with
the Divine blessing, may have the effect of stirring up
your minds by way of remembrance, and stimulating you to
greater zeal and more entire devotedness to the work of the

ministry to which you have been consecrated. Weak as we are in ourselves, and not sufficient for these things, we have the Divine assurance that if we wait on the Lord he will renew our strength; that His grace will be sufficient for us, and that His strength is made perfect in the weakness of those who labour for Him. Relying, then, on the promise of Him who cannot lie, and leaning on the Almighty arm of our reconciled God and Father, let us persevere to sow the good seed of the word, even in the dark and cloudy day, trusting that the Lord will water it with His blessing, and in due time cause it to bring forth fruit to the praise and glory of His name. In the country where many of you will be called to labour, you will find much to try your faith and patience; you will be called to bear many privations and to endure much fatigue and hardship; but I trust you will be enabled to take all these things joyfully, for the love of Christ your Lord, and through zeal for the salvation of immortal souls. Let the consideration that you are the ambassadors of Christ—that you are commissioned by the King of Kings to proclaim a full and free pardon to rebellious man, be ever uppermost in your thoughts. This will sustain you in all trials, and will constrain you unreservedly to devote your-selves to the work of the ministry to which you are called.

You will have many difficulties to contend with, some from the open opposition of the enemies of the Gospel, many from the corruption which still remains in your own flesh, but the greater difficulties, and those which will try you most and longest, will arise from the coldness, the deadness, and the utter indifference to spiritual things, of those to whom you will be called to minister. Prayer is the Christian's resource under such difficulties. The Holy Spirit alone can subdue the unruly wills and affections of sinful men. He alone can break up the fallow ground of the human heart, and prepare it for the reception of the good seed. Oh, for more of the Spirit of Prayer amongst us! The praying minister is the powerful minister. As the face of Moses shone when he was admitted to close personal converse with God upon the mount, so the servant of Christ who frequently holds communion with his God in prayer, will reflect in his character and his life something of the light and likeness of Him in whom all fulness dwells, and out of whose fulness we are privileged to receive even grace for grace.

In conclusion, my Reverend Brethren, I would "commend you to God, and the word of His Grace, which is able to build you up, and to give you an inheritance among all them which are sanctified," study to shew yourselves approved unto God, workmen that need not to be ashamed, rightly dividing the word of truth. Remember that your work is for eternity, and though your labours may not attract the attention or draw forth the praise of men, still you are to proceed, regardless of self, and not setting your hearts upon obtaining the approval of men, or popularity amongst those who love not the Lord Jesus Christ. To be loved, to be highly esteemed by the meek and lowly followers of Christ, should indeed be the desire of every faithful minister of the Lord Jesus; but to labour for the applause of the ungodly and unbelieving, argues a mind yet carnal, and can only be productive of evil both to the minister and to the people. May then the God of all grace, the giver of every good and perfect gift, pour upon you in large measure His Holy Spirit, that you may be faithful, humble, zealous and devoted followers and servants of Christ, and that, when He, the Chief Shepherd shall appear, you may receive the crown of righteousness which fadeth not away.

APPENDIX.

Note A., page 9.

*The following Report of a Committee on Indian Missions was
adopted at the last meeting of the Synod of the Diocese:*

The Committee appointed at the last annual meeting of the
Synod on the subject of Indian Missions beg leave to report:

That as the conversion and civilization of the Gentiles were
a subject of primary consideration with the Christian Church
from the first, so should the long neglected aborigines of this
land be regarded by our Reformed Church with a like solicitude and care for their evangelization and enlightenment.

It is only within the last twenty-five years that the Government of this Province has extended any assistance towards so
desirable an object as the Christian education of some of the
Indian tribes, and it is with regret that your Committee have
learned that the Missionaries employed by the Government
were notified from the Indian Department that after the expi-
ration of the current year, they were to expect no further aid
from this source.

Under these circumstances your Committee are encouraged
to hope that by a timely representation to some of our Church
Societies at home of the peculiar position in which some of the
Indian Missions are about to be placed, they may be induced
to take them up, and so secure the ministrations of the Church
enjoyed by them for some years.

The Committee are happy to state, that some of these Missions have from an early period been favoured with the foster-
ing care and generous support of a company in England, which
renders them comparatively independent of any government
support.

The Indian tribes at present under the charge of Missionaries
of the Church your Committee desire to notice *seriatim*, as well
as the sources whence these have been hitherto maintained.

I. The Six Nations Indians on the Grand River are under the paternal care of the New England Company, which not only provides salaries for Missionaries and Schoolmasters, but also defrays the expenses of an Industrial School, where children are taught, (in addition to the branches of a common English education), the boys, agricultural and useful arts, and the girls, spinning, knitting, and different descriptions of needle-work.

Though a large majority of these Indians have embraced Christianity, and become members of the Church of England, yet a considerable proportion, chiefly of the Cayuga tribes, have for many years rejected the Gospel. The labours of the Company's Missionaries among them have not, however, been altogether in vain : from time to time it pleases God to open the hearts of some of them to attend His Word, and they have lately expressed a wish to have a school established amongst them. A greater number of Schoolmasters, and two additional Missionaries are much needed among the Six Nations. The Mohawk tribe, having surrendered their lands in the vicinity of Brantford to the Government for sale, have removed to a new settlement on the south side of the Grand River, and can no longer, without travelling far too great a distance, assemble for the worship of God in their old Church at the Mohawk village. Little if any thing can for the present be expected from the New England Company towards the erection of a new church, they (however willing to afford assistance) having been lately at much expense in putting up new buildings for the accommodation of a greater number of children at the Mohawk Institution. Your Committee hope that at no very distant period our Church Society will be enabled to contribute to this desirable work.

II. The Muncey and Oneida Indians on the Thames have been under Christian instruction for a number of years. The Missionary who has been labouring among the former tribe for a quarter of a century, found them pagans upon his first visit, since which period it has pleased Almighty God to call them from darkness to the acknowledgment of saving truth as it is in the finished work of redeeming love in a crucified Saviour. Many of the latter tribe, who came into this Province about eighteen years ago from the United States, have attached themselves to the Church of England. The Catechist and Schoolmaster of the Munceys has been in receipt of a salary of £50 per annum from the Church Society of the Diocese of Toronto for the last few years. The Catechist and Schoolmaster of the Oneidas is paid a salary of £50 sterling by the Colonial Church and School Society since his appointment. A small salary to interpreters for the above tribes has been granted also by the Church Society of Toronto, at the rate of £12 10s. currency each, for the last few years.

III. The Ojibwas of Walpole Island have been in charge of a Missionary for a number of years, whose salary was paid partly by the Indian Department, and partly by the Society for the Propagation of the Gospel in Foreign Parts. He has also received notice that his salary is to be discontinued after the present year. The Schoolmaster stationed in this Mission has also been allowed a salary from the funds of the Church Society of Toronto. There are two Sunday services, and also one week-day service, regularly; the congregation at each very good. There is also an excellent Sunday school. The day school is well attended, the number of scholars on the list being sixty-five, and the average daily in attendance throughout the year being thirty-five. Many of the pupils are able to read in the New Testament, some to write very well, others can work sums expertly in the elementary rules of arithmetic, and two or three are acquainted with the general outlines of geography; and most of them, by means of instruction through the week and on Sundays, are more or less acquainted with the elementary truths of Christianity.

IV. The Ojibwas of Owen Sound have been in the enjoyment of Christian instruction for some time, through one of your Missionaries, who is not in receipt of any remuneration whatever for his Indian services. The only assistence afforded this band of Indians is a small allowance by the Church Society of the Diocese of Toronto to their Schoolmaster and Interpreter: this, we learn, will be discontinued.

In addition to the above bands of Indians, there are other tribes within the bounds of the Diocese, to whom the ministrations of our Church have never been extended.

The Committee would respectfully submit the following suggestions, with the view of sustaining and extending the ministrations of the Church among the Indians of Muncey, Oneida, Walpole Island, and Owen Sound, which Missions are now about to be deprived of all Government aid :

That seeing there is no prospect of obtaining any adequate relief in this Province towards the sustentation and efficiency of these Missions, your Committee are of opinion that if a representation of the peculiar position in which these interesting Missions are about to be placed were made by his Lordship the Bishop to some of our Church Societies in England, whose great object it is to send Missionaries to the Pagan, that the same would be attended with the most satisfactory results.

All which is respectfully submitted,

RICHARD FLOOD,
Chairman.

Note B., page 10.

Th following Letter and those referred to in the next two notes were written, by the Missionaries to the Indians, to the Secretary of the Church Society in answer to a Circular addressed to them by direction of the Bishop.

BRANTFORD, *June* 14*th*, 1859.

REV. AND DEAR SIR,

We beg to acknowledge your circular of the 16th May last, requesting us to furnish a statistical account of the Indians under our charge ; as we labour together among the same people, we consider that it will be most satisfactory to make a joint report.

The number of the Six Nations Indians residing at the Grand River is about 2400. It is generally stated that the Indians are rapidly diminishing in numbers in their different settlements, but such is not the case with respect to the Six Nations, who, on the contrary, are gradually on the increase ; and we have every reason to believe that such will be the general result wherever the Indians are protected in the undisturbed possession of their lands. They profess Christianity for the most part, although a large majority of the Cayugas, numbering about 500, together with a few Onondagas, are still pagan.

The Christian portion of the Six Nations Indians are principally members and adherents of the Church of England, and even those who are pagans are friendly to that Church, and almost always unite themselves to it whenever they embrace the Christian religion. The New England Company has for many years furnished the means of religious and secular education, and at present employs among them two clergymen, and several catechists, besides seven schoolmasters. There are repeated applications for more schools, and two additional clergymen are much needed. The number of communicants in connection with the Church of England is about 250, and of children attending the above schools 263. There is a great difficulty in securing regular attendance at the day schools; but at the New England Company's Institution, where the children are boarded and educated, their progress in learning is much more satisfactory. Four of the school teachers at present employed are Indians who have been educated at this Institution, and another, through the liberality of the same Society, is pursuing his studies with a view to entering the ministry.

In addition to the New England Company's missions, the Wesleyan Methodists support a missionary and one schoolmaster among these people.

A few years ago the Indians were induced to give up their farms and improvements on the north side of the river, and remove to another settlement on the south side, in consequence of which they stand in need of a new Church, as the old one, which was the first Episcopal Church erected in Upper Canada, is at too great a distance to be used by them for public worship. As the New England Company, to whom the Indians have been hitherto chiefly indebted for the means of improvement, has incurred a large expense in building a new Institution, and extending its operations among them, its funds will not admit of its contributing to this new object, and it is very desirable that for this purpose funds should be obtained from some other source.

The country adjacent to the Indian reserve being now in the occupation of white settlers, the Six Nations are deprived of

F

the means of subsistence by hunting, fishing, &c., and unlike many other tribes, are turning their attention very much to agriculture. They are mostly settled upon separate lots of land, and although labouring under the hardships always attending a new settlement, many of them have made large improvements, and raise considerable grain; and although the characteristic improvidence of the Indian is very visible among them, yet there is a great improvement in this respect. Many erect comfortable houses and good barns, and take better care of their cattle during winter than formerly.

A too easy access to places where ardent spirits are sold has been a hindrance to the improvement of the Six Nations, and some have been much addicted to drinking; but, as a body, they are far from being more given to excess than the white population, and of late years evince great aversion, and frequently are active in opposition to intemperance in the settlement.

We remain,

Rev. and dear Sir,

Your obedient servants,

AB'M NELLES.
A. ELLIOT.

THE REV. J. W. MARSH,
Ingersoll, C. W.

Note C., page 10.

WALPOLE ISLAND MISSION,
27th May, 1859.

MY DEAR SIR,

I received your kind letter, informing me that it was the intention of his Lordship the Bishop to bring the state of the Indians in this Diocese before such Societies as his Lordship will think likely to assist us in our work amongst the Indians, and that it is desirable that I should furnish a statistical return of the Indians under my charge, with an account of their state, their prospects and their wants. In acordance with the Bishop's request, I send you the following narrative—thankful that the Lord has put it into the heart of our Bishop to make an effort on behalf of the poor Indians, now that the Government has withdrawn from us its aid.

The Mission on Walpole Island has been in existence 18 years—having been opened in 1811. I was appointed to the Mission by the late Lord Metcalfe, on the 17th June, 1845, and have thus been connected with it during a period of nearly fourteen years. Two Missionaries preceded me, but these, owing to certain untoward circumstances, met with no success in converting the natives. In the summer of 1845 the Walpole Islanders were immersed in the degradation of barbarism. They worshipped and offered sacrifices to evil spirits, practised witchcraft, were polygamists. The waubannoo, the pagan dance, the tricks of the conjuror, were in full swing. With the exception of a few small patches of Indian corn, tilled very imperfectly, they paid no attention to the cultivation of the soil. They had no oxen, no cows. The hoe was the only farming implement they possessed. For food they depended mainly on hunting. They were exceedingly lazy and apathetic, and betook themselves to the chase only when impelled by hunger or some other necessity, and after obtaining the wished for venison, they would return to their wigwams, and as long as the supply lasted would enjoy themselves after their fashion, in feasting, in dancing, and in drinking the fire-water. They had no thought of the morrow, and cared for nothing but present enjoyment. They were indolent and most averse to labour, and might have been seen at any hour of the day stretched out on the grass, sleeping off the effects of a drunken debauch. They verified to the letter the old Indian motto, " It is better to walk than to run, it is better to stand than to walk, it is better to sit than to stand, it is better to lie than to sit."

It would indeed be difficult to conceive of a more dissipated, poor, miserable set of beings than those Islanders were in 1845. I will never forget the feeling of despondency which came over me during the first few months of my residence on the Island. Their reformation seemed impossible, and no small degree of faith was necessary to enable me to believe that any improvement could take place amongst so degraded and superstitious a people. But what seemed impossible to man was possible to God.

At first the Indians were remarkably shy, and it was only after a long course of uniform kindness that I succeeded in gaining their attention. During the first year I had no congregation; the Church bell, of course, was rung, and regular hours for service were appointed, but only now and then an Indian would venture into Church. At length, in July, 1846, two were baptized. These I call the first fruits of Walpole Island. They are still living—both hold fast their profession, and one of them, named Thomas Buckwheat, has been of great service to me in bringing over to Christianity his brethren of the tribe. Up to the present time I have received into the Church 350 Indians. The whole number of communicants is 56. The Sunday congregations are excellent, and it is delightful to witness their quiet and becoming deportment during Divine Service. The change in the condition of these Indians is obviously very great. Formerly Sunday in their eyes was no better than any other day, and from my own door I have often seen them on that holy day, fishing, or ploughing, planting corn, or having a horse race, or perhaps, what was still worse, sitting in groups by the river side enjoying a pagan jollification. Now all this, I am happy to say, is changed. There has, indeed, been no sudden rush of success, the improvement in their condition has been slow and gradual, and, on that account, likely to be lasting. The Sunday is honoured and kept as a Christian Sabbath. Many of them dress neatly, and come to Church in a quiet, orderly manner, and many of them, I have reason to believe, understand, appreciate, and are influenced by the saving doctrines of the Gospel. Paganism, however, has still many votaries on the Island, but these persons have been influenced indirectly by the good examples of the Christians around them; they are now more orderly, more industrious, and less dissipated than before, and are likely at no distant day to be won over to the profession and the blessings of Christianity.

The Indians have made considerable advances in the social scale. They have a decided aptitude for the mechanical trades. Many of them are rough carpenters and blacksmiths, and some of them are competent to build a house, or execute the interior or pannelled work in a manner which would do credit to a professional tradesman.

Their progress in temporal matters has been marked and decided. No band of Indians in Canada West, considering the time they have been under the care of Missionaries, have made greater progress in habits of industry and self-reliance. I send you the subjoined extract from the Report of the Commissioners appointed by the Government to visit the several Indian Stations throughout Canada. (See Report, page 57.) The number of acres on the Island, cleared, amount to 2,139, and the produce raised there by the Indians, in the last year (1857) was as follows :—

Wheat......(bushels)	1,517	Peas ....(bushels)	377
Corn ... .. "	6,388	Potatoes...... "	3,965
Oats ...... "	547	Buckwheat "	74
Beans ...... "	418	Hay ....(tons)	294

They have no regular village, but live more or less scattered on their several clearings. They have 4 frame and 94 log houses, while 41 families still live in wigwams. They have, besides, 28 barns, of which 6 are frame buildings, the remainder being constructed of logs. Their live stock, to the raising of which they pay considerable attention, consists of

Cows	75	Young Horses	150
Yokes of Oxen	41	Pigs..........................	514
Young Cattle............	132	Sheep	11
Horses............................	179		

Their farming implements are the same as those in use among the whites, and comprise

Waggons	9	Harrows	23
Carts................., ...	3	Fanning Mills	7
Sleighs	46	Thrashing Machines	1
Sets of Harness	56	Sets of Carpenter's Tools..	9
Ploughs ...., ...	48	Sets of Blacksmith's Tools	1

The frame barns were erected entirely at the cost of the owners, and during the last year four good log houses have been completed with but small assistance from the Indian Department. The whole of the work was done by the Indians.

There are at present on the Island,—

Members of the Church of England 230
Methodists.................................. 53
Roman Catholics 19
Pagans 522

The above statistics are taken from the published Report of the Commissioners who visited this Mission in the summer of 1857.

As is the case in many other Missions, I am not only a Missionary, but feel obliged often to act in the capacity of a Physician, Schoolmaster, Interpreter, and, not unfrequently, as a quasi-Magistrate, in short, I have had to make myself useful in a variety of ways. The small-pox, that deadly foe of the Indian, has visited the Island during my residence here, and all who were attacked by it died. Under the blessing of a kind Providence, its further progress was arrested by timely vaccination. Nearly 300 of the natives were vaccinated by my wife. Christians, Pagans, Conjurers, Medicine Men, old and young, flocked to the Mission House to obtain the antidote, and though several years have passed away since then, they often express gratitude to the white squaw.

Much of my attention has been given to the acquirement of the language. On my arrival, I knew nothing of it, but now I converse in it easily, and it is no small pleasure to be able to talk to my people, to counsel them, to reprimand them, or encourage them without the intervention of an interpreter. This power, of course, was not acquired without great labour. I have given my days and nights to the study of the Chippawa, and often in the early part of my career I would remain in their wigwams, seated on their mats for hours, watching them and listening to their conversation. My labour in this respect has not been lost, for I can now speak to them in their own tongue, of the unsearchable riches of Christ.

There is a very good school on the Island, taught by an Indian, a steady and respectable person, and who, in a great measure, has been educated by myself. He delights in teaching, and several of his pupils have made respectable progress. Many of the youth read easily in the New Testament, others write beautifully—good penmanship being easily acquired by

Indians; some are also able to cast accounts with expertness and accuracy, a few also are acquainted with the general outlines of geography, and are pretty well posted up in the mountains, lakes, and large rivers in the grand divisions of the earth's surface. And all of them, from the instructions given them during the day school, and especially at Sunday school, are more or less acquainted with the fundamental truths of Christianity.

The Indians, from the age of 25 and upwards, are unable to read, and yet many of them who have joined the Church are familiar with different portions of the Prayer Book, and make the responses devoutly and intelligently. Their knowledge of it was acquired in this way : while giving instruction to the young converts, I encouraged them to commit to memory portions of the Liturgy, and this they were enabled to do by my reading them over and over again to them. By this method they became acquainted with the Confession, the Lord's Prayer, the Creed, the Ten Commandments, with the Psalms in metre and Hymns. My plan was to read the Psalms or Hymns over line by line, verse by verse, and never to pass on to a second verse until the first had been thoroughly mastered. The constant reading of the same lines, dozens of times over at a sitting, was often very irksome ; but my labour was repaid by the slow and sure proficiency of my pupils, and in witnessing their delight when they had mastered another psalm or hymn. They would say " Now this is beautiful. Now this is ours for ever. When in church, or when alone, or when in sickness, we can think of these lines and become wise and happy."

Amongst the Psalms, the 23rd and 51st are especial favourites with our Indians. They are also very fond of the Morning and Evening Hymn. The Prayer Book in use here is the translation made by Dr. O'Meara. The Indians and the Church at large owe a debt of gratitude to him for his able and faithful translation of the Liturgy and New Testament, both of which are used here, and are highly valued. It would have pleased the Doctor, and I am sure it would have been some slight recompense to him for his labour of love, to have heard our Indians exclaim, when I read to them some psalm or hymn for the first time, "How sweet that is! How very comforting! How much like God!" The Doctor paid us a visit two or three years ago, and preached to large and attentive congregations. He is a great favourite here, and goes by the name of the "Uhyawpechenhnishenaubamood;" in English, "The great Indian speaker," or, still more literally, "He who speaks Indian thoroughly."

I am thankful that a fresh effort is about to be made on behalf of this people, and I shall await the result of his Lordship's appeal to the Societies in England with no little anxiety. The Indians are still poor; their annuity is the smallest, I am told, received by any Chippawa band in the country, for if equally divided amongst them it would not much exceed one dollar per head. The sick and the needy amongst them naturally look to the Missionary for aid, but what can he do if he be in semi-poverty himself? I have spent on Walpole Island the flower of my days, and I never dreamt that after devoting my best energies to the welfare of its inhabitants, that the imperial grant could possibly be withdrawn from me. I came here under the impression that the support promised me would be continued to the end—at least so long as I continued a Missionary amongst the Indians. It appears that I have been mistaken. Nehertheless, I still keep up courage, and cling to the hope that my long cherished idea will be realized—to live and die an Indian Missionary.

Yours faithfully,

ANDREW JAMIESON.

To the Rev. J. WALKER MARSH, A.M.,
    Sec. Ch. Soc. Diocese of Huron, Ingersoll, C. W.

Note D., page 10.

DELAWARE, *May* 26, 1859.

My DEAR SIR,—In reply to your late circular expressive of the desire of the Lord Bishop, that I should furnish you with some details in reference to the Indians embraced within my charge, it may prove interesting to his Lordship to be made acquainted with some particulars connected with my Mission amongst them, &c.

Shortly after my arrival in this Province in the year 1833, I discovered the Muncey tribe of Indians, exceeding two hundred, at that time all Pagans, residing on the river Thames, about ten miles distant from the village of Delaware, whom I could then only reach by an Indian trail, or intricate pathway through the forest.

Now as the white settlers in the townships of Delaware and Caradoc under my ministry did not exceed one hundred families, I was induced to devote a portion of my time, that of every other week, to those long neglected aborigines. Since that period this entire band of Indians have not only renounced paganism, and embraced the Christian faith as professed by our Reformed Church, but many of them have continued " to walk worthy of their high calling and profession," adorning the doctrine of Christ their Saviour by a holy life and blameless conversation.

This labour of love, I would remark, under a deep sense of responsibility, was undertaken without any remuneration or most distant prospect of it. I had a mission house built, in the year 1835, in the village Delaware, and rafted down the river to their village, in order to enable me to reside among them occasionally with the view of arresting their attention to the all saving truths of the Gospel, as set forth in the fulness, freeness and completeness of the redemption which is by faith in Christ only.

It was not until some years afterwards that a small allowance was made me at the instance of Sir Geo. Arthur, Lieut. Governor, who having learned that some success attended my labours, expressed a desire to learn more particulars in detail in reference to my Mission to the Indians, which I communicated to him ; and the same, he was pleased to say, afforded him much satisfaction and pleasure.

I consider the Munceys, both mentally and physically, a very superior race compared with other tribes of Indians. They are industrious and sober, with very few exceptions, and I can assure you that my spirit has been often cheered and comforted by witnessing the Christian consistency and uprightness of conduct in many of the poor Munceys.

G

They are not like other tribes in receipt of land payments from the Government, as they came into this Province from the United States during the American war as the free and independent allies of Great Britain, and have since been residing on a Chippaway reserve by sufferance. Had their fathers applied for lands after the close of the war, there can be little doubt but their request would have been granted. Their staple as to living, principally consists of corn, besides which they raise some wheat, oats, and potatoes, sufficient for their families. They are also in possession of a considerable number of cattle, and are generally more comfortable in their circumstances than the tribes which are in receipt of money yearly for lands surrendered to the Crown.

The Oneidas came into this Province also about eighteen years since from the State of New York, U. S., and purchased lands a few miles distant from the Munceys, on the river Thames, with the money which they received for the sale of their lands to the United States Government. Soon after their arrival in Canada I learned from conversation with some of them that they originally belonged to the Episcopal Church of the U. S., but that after a large portion of their tribe had sold out and left many years before this period for Green Bay, in Illinois, U. S., this party was left without a spiritual instructor, and in consequence thereof many of them joined the Methodists. This was precisely their religious position when they came to this country, with the exception of six families which were and still remain pagans.

Some of their chiefs, who still valued the services of our Church, and were confirmed by the Bishop of New York, expressed a wish that I should extend my ministrations to them, with which request I gladly complied. Those in connexion with our Church built a comfortable school-house at their own expense, which also answers the purpose of a temporary church, that can accommodate over one hundred worshippers. The average attendance ranges about seventy. This tribe musters about 450, 150 of whom profess attachment to our Church. Among them are some excellent farmers, together with some mechanics. William Doxtater, the head chief of the Church party, raises a large quantity of grain every year, of which he sells from two to three hundred bushels. There are many others equally industrious.

Many, however, in this tribe are poor through their own indolence; and I regret to say that there are some of the young men, especially, who are intemperate in their habits.

It has been my experience to record the hopeful deaths of many in these tribes, who have departed this life in the sure and certain hope of a happy resurrection unto eternal life through Jesus Christ our Lord.

Captain Snake, the head chief, and first fruits to Christ among the Munceys, was a striking instance of the power of sovereign grace from the commencement of his Christian career to the last hour of his earthly course; as were also the Hawks, the Halfmoons, the Logans, with many like minded, over whom I could rejoice as those who have exchanged an earthly for an heavenly inheritance.

As salaries must be provided for Indian Missionaries after the current year in consequence of the withdrawal of Government assistance, I hope that some of our Missionary Societies in our Fatherland will come to the rescue of the poor Indians, and continue to them the ministrations of our Church which they have so long enjoyed.

It would be desirable, also, that some small fund should be created for the purpose of purchasing cotton-yarn, &c., in order that the Indian girls at our schools might be instructed in needle-work, under the instruction of our schoolmasters' wives.

I am about making an experiment on a small scale at my Oneida school, through the kind superintendence of Mrs. Potts, by supplying them with some materials for needle-work.

I remain, yours faithfully,
RICHARD FLOOD.

To the Rev. J. W. Marsh, M.A.,
    &c.,   &c.,   &c.

Note E., page 10.

The name of the Diocese—"Huron"—was adopted at the suggestion of the Hon. G. J. Goodhue, as the new Diocese comprised the hunting ground of the Hurons, whose council fires had for ages lighted up all parts of these western forests.